ELLE: A VERSE NOVEL

Robert Sheppard has published numerous volumes of prose and poetry, creative and critical, fiction and non-fiction, has been widely anthologised and published in dozens of magazines and journals, over 50 years. Emeritus Professor of Poetry and Poetics at Edge Hill University, he lives in Liverpool, though he was born on the South Coast, where, before university in Norwich, his adolescent surrealism was first nurtured, and he was introduced to the radical British poetry of the day, to which he remains committed.

Also by Robert Sheppard

British Standards	(Shearsman, 2024)
The Necessity of Poetics	(Shearsman, 2024)
Doubly Stolen Fire	(Aquifer, 2023)
Bad Idea	(Knives Forks and Spoons, 2021)
The English Strain	(Shearsman, 2021)
Micro Event Space	(Red Ceilings, 2019)
Unfinish	(Veer, 2016)
The Meaning of Form in Contemporary Innovative Poetry	(Palgrave, 2016)
History or Sleep: Selected Poems	(Shearsman, 2015)
Words Out of Time	(Knives, Forks and Spoons, 2015)
A Translated Man	(Shearsman, 2013)
Berlin Bursts	(Shearsman, 2011)
When Bad Times Made for Good Poetry	(Shearsman, 2011)
Warrant Error	(Shearsman, 2009)
Complete Twentieth Century Blues	(Salt, 2008)
The Poetry of Saying: British Poetry and its Discontents 1950-2000	(Liverpool University Press, 2005)
The Lores	(Reality Street, 2003)
Far Language: Poetics and Linguistically Innovative Poetry 1978-1997	(Stride, 1999)
Empty Diaries	(Stride, 1998)
The Flashlight Sonata	(Stride, 1993)
Daylight Robbery	(Stride, 1990)
Returns	(Textures, 1985)

CONTENTS

ISBN: 978-1-917617-47-5

Cover designed by Aaron Kent

Edited and Typeset by Aaron Kent

Broken Sleep Books Ltd
PO BOX 102
Llandysul
SA44 9BG

Elle

Robert Sheppard

Broken Sleep Books

PREFACE

'Write a preface,' people commented. Tragedy chose my subject as a healthy order of *her* love for mental-sensual aberration. It came across clear, especially what I did not mean.

ONE: HARNESS ON A MAN'S THICK FIRM FIGURE

Reins apart, Harvey Holford loved his stirrups.
Christine Holford was holding forward, only to reach
the open street of smiling girls in sledges. Her body:
too heavy for the tow with absolutely no risk.
Come swung lightly as quiver
was used tightly with her feet first time,
her facial defects squared. She felt
balanced ground. She could fool all the way,
this time of day, sporting friends.

Passing the night club, Christine stumbled
for a living creature. Her love smiled,
her breast tanned, harmony assured.
Holford had everything across his face,
curves of clouds on the slopes. He turned grey.
Marvellous snow-covered artificial summits,
the wind skating! Fleece-grace: Holford's
trot thrill! They went, feeling into confidence.
Her muscles met heavy sledges. Faces sat on voice-time.
Christine called this happiness. Christine
from inside already told the noble roadway
her balance. Rhythm stopped thinking.

The rhythm of herself ruled. Her body
was no longer impetuous:
'I see Holford made one happy swing.'
The road couldn't make it, half buried
in an icy trickle down her standing up.
Christine ended ignoring Holford.
They pulled a rest. He suggested being shown
to place, scrubbed and scrubbed his own
character. 'You can breathe in everything.
The people say you love me for my voice.'
With his lips, the waitress disappeared rapidly,
brushed her cheese.

Hungry gorge turns the fragile halo's perched
spindles: a startlingly black waistcoat.
'The females know perfectly well when you scowl.
Darling, I love Harvey.' Christine could see all
the moods that touched her snowball chuck.
His mouth replied in a fierce battle. In the face
they were embroiled, the embarrassed smile.
A somewhat motherly Christine remounted him.
Their lungs occupied adjoining rooms.
'Have a good shivering,' she cried, 'rub a little instinct.'

Sharp, as if it had come from solicitude,

Christine felt cold. Cheeks burning impatiently,

she went, 'That was a beautiful black body.'

Holford moulded her firm: stood, kissed,

stroked her gesture-head. The young woman

spotted Heather Thatcher, her vivacious Viennese

friend, bursting with surgeon-affection for Christine:

'I'm over Germans, our horse took a lovely blue cocktail.'

'English feels foreign,' Holford said, coming back.

'You want a drink, Bloom?' Champagne minds murmured.

John Bloom kissed Heather's touch.

Christine's disagreeable face on his admired fingers,

pleasant enough, endowed with heavenly immobility.

Watch the others think without a skating daresay.

Voice his features, captivate his musical power:

'Girls! Half a dozen. No, just the one! A big Danish!'

'*Scarf!*' squawked Christine, hips like Holford. A

naked look, a jersey besides. He touched his fine

clothes, chilly hands purely erotic, obscene.

Bloom chaste women. 'What made the beauties

of our bad taste?' *His* words (in other words).

Thought interrupted combinations

of nightclub barmaid attire. Excited Heather said,

'I'm only a little alcoholic.' Holford left his things, said,

'Realise, Bloom!', suddenly not too bad after Christine,

seeing his wife's shape. 'Life's ridiculous –

now openly disconcert me; I'm frightened

by an interrupted beat.' His Saltdean rival asked the time.

Talking exhausted him that evening. Christine said,

'Avoid him. He's something from those old cold weeks.

Voices inside you note we've only stopped in Brighton.'

'Your poor trusting excuses. My darling, avoid him,

avoid him! Harvey, make friends of your charms!

Heather will think anything of you. That's a sure sign

we can't be caught. *Darling*,

money's a bad taste in your win. Your race

never thought you'd watch him with Jewish actors

brought up on Shakespeare.' The moonlit play had put him on.

She loved Holford's nobility. 'All forms involve us

sensually,' he murmured, 'in madness and art.'

CHAPTER SWITZERLAND

Christine Holford felt Brighton. Her
husband's hand turned her head, but Christine
wanted self-sufficient exclusive egoism:
her wasted fingernails! Desire spent her blue veins
and Harvey Holford; her husband's body was
an abundant stream of blood. She measured her face.
Her body even imagined daily revival, how she felt
for her great and gentle sensual secret.
Pneumonia was a severe death, by leeches,
her bedside step in her death stupor. One
unrecognisably hot morning, she awoke frightfully –
but the figure was thought without a bedside,
its name only a vague forehead.

A mixture of thoughts discovered the wave
on Christine's stripped everything. Holford
loved those moments that reduced, it seemed,
Christine's joy. Her look: the sick state of pure tender fever.
Crippled, she walked again in the flat. Christine
was Holford's order. For illness she created things,
abstracted light. Life appeared assured:
discipline she smiled. In Sussex, learning nothing,

Holford thought of his 'reveries dim'. Demand
reached beyond something, his existence better
once, as if the same. She played some pensive queer.

That man's having thought-hostility:
came *perfectly* well. Come
with attention pleased her, revived her thoughts
and lips every day. Holford pictured
shuddered Heather Thatcher! John Bloom's revulsion
came to take off her hours. A second frivolity
dizzied her back into makeup, chained her pretty good.
'Love affairs are *moments*!' Christine raged,
mechanically. Vivacity brought such moments, her fingers
strong, automatic, but *not* like attitude. Christine
told Heather, 'Pause him. Surprise him. I'd remember so
much, if it had not been for meeting *him*.'

'Realising you can speak,
I should have explained…
you'd have understood?'
fumbling Christine asked freely.
'Perverse, he's almost done too well,
loathing my words, weirdly to ruin my opposite.
Dangerous others said I couldn't.'
[...]

He wanted to thrill Christine

where she had been seated. He broke Christine's opposite,

determined ease to one side. She shifted

when he was at himself. 'He seldom leaves home.

Who comes bold? He's handsome, I'm sure.'

Invaluable Christine abruptly uttered thanks to Christine.

Whining, he used to start. 'Smell her laugh

which,' he said, 'changes her irrational anxiety.

You've lost yourself: I didn't come to arrange

this stand. Lie down!' She rose beside her tyres,

said she pushed some neat tart before her illness,

Christine easily in order.

Nothing became embarrassed. How softly

movement from the lying down relaxed his only power,

his lethal hearing. Softened while speaking,

Christine could voice now, directed, sat

by her language, cell strength insinuating, 'I was a bit.'

Voluptuousness rolled on her shoulders;

she was amazed in knowing how. Pleasure-disgust

in herself. Saying 'Rape' in those seconds, and 'No',

she stared at barriers, feelings. Christine said finally,

'The gods have felt neutral repugnance.'

[...]

Bloom felt surprise yield to him. She thought
of Holford: she had no stranger to fill.
Her husband's step was going to tell
him. Boredom entered Holford.

He kissed Christine towards her questions.
She stumbled lifeless, obviously trying.
Actually, any number she had then seemed
to keep eyes, given his face, though
he was anguished. 'Darling' started quivering.
His hand at work knew the attempt
about his work. Holford detailed a cult.
His load was no way a low operation.
The little Italian didn't; he died to
answer estrangement. 'Melt softly,' he thought,
as his swept-out tenderness murmured:
'Her immediate sweet maternal head is your
fault. Arms mustn't realise: *you're life*!'

CHAPTER WOKE

Christine Holford, fresh,

was stopped by her body. First

thoughts lay beside her since her

illness. Nightmare protected Harvey

Holford. He had delicious rapture!

Giving herself, she forgot his pleasure –

not by herself a desire to enjoyment.

Convalescence had never known such virgin

disappointment, Christine felt immediately.

Brushed, she saw tenderness early. Holford

deeply passed through Holford. Noble lines,

sleeping two years like the rich, always.

Virtuous mistakes of the will and the means:

both honest hands smile. 'Peace,' thought Christine,

drug-evoked by any-health. Her need, their love,

Holford's shining moment of 'Mercy'. (Holford

did not understand the word and that worked,

curiously.) Dark, she was against good.

She *thought* anxiety, the idea mixed

only with Holford. She loved

the assurance within her. What a boy

in her hands, his days never knew!

Christine felt so simple at that moment: hot,

impulsive, perfect power believed quickly.

Christine's balance discouraged her

emotion. Possession lay dormant

in her secret. Introspection controlled

her imagined idea of no hold over personality-desires.

Christine had this result of her reason

which she could wait no longer to show.

She kissed his state body! Holford pressed

her warm voice. Christine switched on

total felicity. The woman murmured light.

Her light spread Holford, who belonged

to the shadows: Christine had his features

again, mysterious semblance, now wonderful.

Suddenly he continued, 'Christine! Stroke my pain!

I'm too full of else hush!' He was calm.

'Have you been feeling Christine? Better

think about those long sleeping rôles!' She said:

'I ask you, how there was my husband's kind?'

She stopped, surprise face. 'Please,' he muttered,

'don't be continued! Your operation in Holford's

feelings.' He imagined a sort of *now*.

[...]

The slightest crime lost control
of his anxious 'darling'. Love took
against her, to share however much she wanted.
His reading to Christine felt cultured,
continual confusion, 'darling',
Holford suddenly discovering.

So well, so often played, so proudly, she must surely
at that moment have gleamed. Before her ecstasy, arms
round her more. Taken without moving, Holford
had not loved; his mis-aroused thinking loved *him*.
Sensuality made of this woman his life,
religiously a dull misery. Christine herself felt total power
over a soul that belonged to *her* soul. Her own body
was thick with passionate, essential love.
They soothed everything. Christine slipped
her innocent companion – some life their love was!

Sensuality: a rarer daylight of the instincts' flame,
mysterious dark Holford. Christine pitiless to faces,
other-primed for the night, said, 'Come
to the sick room. All over now. Hurry up!'
Holford told her about his decided time.
(I thought it best to conceal this.)

CHAPTER EXORCISED WOMAN

Christine Holford felt unknown. On the brink
of succession, she accepted sickness. Corrupt
fantasies quit this creature, strong for the shades
of that once-more world resumed, the normal place
in this straightforward 'before'. Pleasures restored
the details of one room, her desire-inflections,
her vitality on a voyage with deep functional servants.
She was *feelings*. Vigour never had Harvey Holford.
Christine: her sickness was happiness, seductive tenderness
of the imperfect husband's frustration. Disturbed,
Holford swung.

Christine kept the same happy appetite for
everything. New clothes chose girlish *couturiers*.
Hat-shops prevented her worrying about
Heather Thatcher in these shopping cutters,
faultless paraphernalia too quickly fitting. It showed
Christine always tempted Heather's evening. Business help
was due eventually. Already 'darling' glanced
at Christine's *vendeuse*. 'You comment on something,
Valerie? Tea party to a night club,' went on:
'There's Valerie, she talks a lot, slander secret.'
[...]

'Christine, believe me. Listen to all the doubts.'

'Do you think I'm afraid?'

'Mademoiselle' gave meticulous instructions:

she will rule at the fitting. Christine

realised one over Heather: Holford will come!

Valerie Hatcher went on, 'No, that couple!'

Another thought met the whole idea.

(You know at most that's not even words.)

'Darling stranger, don't dress.' The night club

mechanically said nothing. *A night club?* The Calypso?

The Blue Gardenia? She second guessed it, her excitement

exclaimed this world, strongly as harm.

(One only thought *imagine the mercy of it!*)

Doing what he wanted with total strangers,

everything, every day: 'Imagine darling,

imagine yourself a night club hostess

expatiated on silence, in order to draw

Christine's terrified mould.' She failed.

Frigid Christine seemed impossible;

the limbs moved but she was never anguished

before her contorted lids. Unspeakable flames

could see naked with her fingers, but her hands

screamed each loathsome image as the rest of her body would.

Her friends took Christine to lodge vitality

out of a scarlet Pontiac Parisienne –

only returned with a sudden shock. Her affection

in the icy mystery of her stupor

thought she was staring. She

became aware of a mechanism-stranger.

This woman wanted to detach possession.

She explained this person with excruciating

hollow eyes to escape her fascination towards

its imperative image: bulging lifeless lips

and bestiality! Pouting panic was a second ground

as frightful door handles locked herself.

Between herself and the mirror,

she realised she had a face – and honesty.

She said aloud, 'Pride!' Christine shut anything

that might reflect a chair. She pressed her cold hands

to think chaotic impulses of her desperate state.

Animal-mask Christine emerged from shame.

She did so to rally the dim. She groaned.

She had the depths of her soul opposed.

Will power prevented her quickly.

[...]

Holford's den strove to black anything.

On the telephone, Christine said to Heather,

'I must have barely...' She breathed...

She hadn't to ask herself, she just didn't know.

Christine short-hoped that Heather would say,

'Absolutely mention it to Harvey.' 'I'm not spring,

you know.' 'Don't wear it so impatiently.'

Christine became clear of her sole motive.

Heather heard Holford come. Inexplicable fear

gripped him. It must have been at least ten

minutes' bewilderment: I still have her minutes.

'Ask Heather but don't imagine!' She sensed

every word could not have explained a minute.

'Life, take my things off!' Still bearing the nature

of her guilty excuses, she lurked in her husband,

masculine enemy crouching, fully aware of dementia.

Touch done. An evening of some power, healthily upset.

Security efforts of despotic Christine felt Holford quarrel.

(I was disappointed that this was the only decided

resolution, everything she threw back into lived blazing,

like enjoying herself by the idea alone.) The variety *did* give

her suspension over the street. Agony filled her splashes.

[...]

Speaking gossip, Christine, shot flat,

was rather upset: '*A night club*?'

Christine summoned the strength to slake her thirst.

She wanted to like them. Heather said,

'I had no idea as every Other. You would be boys!'

'I'm jealous, that's all. Do you want Valerie

frightened about something in the world? Let's talk

about drug sensation as the addict's needle

pricks her expectations, snatched!' Holford

lacked substance, and thought fingers spread a single cell.

'Her breasts tell me!' she cried. Her words ended

in shoulders. Christine stroked his anxiety.

He saw her standing like a moment of love.

Her stranger exhausted the night. 'How pale's my bed

till Christine in the half-light, turning, leaned

over her face. What is it?' He'd gone to sleep,

not his first vigil by far. Holford had heavy-hearted

eyes. He could bear rigidity in her shivering.

'I'm scared. I'm here. Oh, Harvey, very well,

tell yourself they're stars wearing white eyes.'

Christine was shadowed by tennis balls.

[...]

Now haunted, John Bloom had quietly
accepted coming across Christine. She pretended.
Yet talking to him, Christine only had, for ease,
Bloom's strange show when she rebuffed him.
Quite clearly, gossip went *into* Valerie. Spicy woman
compliments a man, exacting her desires and fantasies.
Christine's interesting toneless want:
the most degrading limited society Christine
hardly ever bent, her limbs continued. Bloom was
into those! That smell of human body was really humility!

'I'm speaking high prices. The same
modest ruin or I'll never go there,
the Royal Pavilion taking its slaves,
food for Bloom. Faceless façade
without any imagination.' Shapeless desire
abiding this but she isolated that blind link.
That moment tortured Christine, for she herself
was not the wall of the subsoil. Her soul
collapsed the ordered world in which they had
open power. She had the pressure of instinct
to measure. She was united with all the days
required of her deep sleep this side of existence.
The words noticed she *lived*, but she transfixed

one single fantasy, the same Daydream

which her initial convalescence had followed.

She was in a face-sudden district: she could hear

his agony. She was sensual during the man –

but the man was painting nameless little angles.

After her 'theme' of two days' blind alley

near the milk bar –The Whisky a Go-Go, of course –

Christine sought her supremely important

secret imaginings that now came back. One

grouped for the man in Holford. She dressed

herself as a scarlet Pontiac. 'Take me

to the street slowly; I've forgotten the quays.'

Christine saw them not so tight; they were slowing

down the odd-numbered side. The driver began

scanning house fronts. Christine knew those

shoulders of acquiescent women anywhere.

She had a tired-looking neck like that

sworn to understanding embarrassment.

Hard lust told Christine

she had food for the man, a painful sense

of silhouette, his arms short. Her home.

His coarse women took flesh and vision

in their urgent 'first time'. Christine's mind

sometimes had to *see*, driven frightened

little signs against brutal lust. Sometimes

themselves again, the next time, they dared to stop

by the door. Even she brushed sad,

made out of sign, the third lettering

on the fourth time. She got up in an open doorway.

She found looking wanted to help. A breath

can live animal on the little wallpaper.

The dark quilt began good humouredly:

'You want to help here? Butter on your nice upkeep?'

'You have the look of ushered come!' Peter Corvell said,

taking Christine through to a huge bed covered with honey.

CHAPTER: HUSBAND

Five nice words understood,

she reached The Royal Pavilion:

its simplicity turned her head, Peter

Corvell overwhelmed at the noble façade

for a second. The sight barred Harvey Holford

from West Pier. One bus remembered his

remarking pleasure palaces, husband palaces,

confusion blindly overlooking Shoreham Harbour.

Southwick delighted the wife who whirled.

Perspectives leaned, could breathe mud:

Christine Holford rolled down its unusual colour,

went down to Shoreham Beach; cut off

from scrap, sludgy sluggishly, she had water, plunged

instantly. She had existence – houseboats, these walls –

and Christine went into it! Men

walked thicker in muddy water.

She had desired nothing. Suddenly

filth in that muddy ooze. It was true,

she had Holford and the implacable Jeff Keen

for that. He would simply pity compassion.

Dragged, she knew him contemptuous. How did

one punish an act of sickness? The cure

with your insane Corvell? *It*:

a complete atom of mouth-close.

Christine's ability to think had left her, sucked

a man in her feverish bare neck to touch her.

She had a boatman, his blue smock:

he stank of Fishersgate. Strength

stared thickly by his own desire. Bored

and uncomfortable, *pure* desire hunted

her down. This was *Encountered Dreams*.

The same hand yearned for Jeff Keen. It.

He had contact, he would not dare thought.

Clarity eyes registered in closed gripping

dissent, and the rubble unloaded loins.

Control the animal. His huge

down forehead – strong, but thirsty.

Another flesh could have the spasm:

the boatman had bound up the world.

'And I had no time that moment

since "it" was insufferable.' *It*.

This man-blind agony of just a minute

vanished and Christine felt 'it' too, her power-time.

She moaned meeting 'it' on Queen's Road.

[...]

She said, 'He shook his thought.'

The inhuman money dug deep in her bag.

The man looked up Christine to street level.

The old decided the direction of the milk bar.

Holford would meet her there, before the past

immediately became a pendulum. Christine's

imperative, a sudden swing: it swung towards

her! Holford completely did 'it', appalling

from being an excuse. Jeff Keen had set the

boatman to do everything. The accident made up

her pretext for any street corner, these city people

did fated sacrifice. Animals didn't know her horror.

She would bring accomplished women he loved

when the milk bar, The Whisky a Go-Go, put on his knot,

the last time consumed. 'Christine, look,

there he is, crossing the white coats.'

She knew little but a strong desire for knowledge.

By the porch, the young man drew near

Christine. Intellectual vigour she dared not call

softly by the instinct of wife. Love was shaded

a few words to her precious features. She then

hungrily examined them, still marked teachers.

[...]

Students love a leader. One unknown world

saw signs of workmen together. The lines

left the look of a man caught with a sacred

red of disturbing smile. She couldn't be angry

with him since they never lunch. 'I happen

to be Holford, in a way, quite unusual

when you make me show you off.' 'With you?'

'With you! Why, everyone's here to hide their pallor.'

Christine crept into her cheeks. 'A second stay

with you felt drawn towards the garden. I would have

lunch.' Christine took spring, innocent beside the back streets;

always in Brighton: the unhealthy pallid children.

Lost workmen. April clouds in the mystery

of benches down the Old Steine. The gargoyle,

old, was visible, strolled, sheltered the timbre

of something else. Arms through the gardens

under the Pavilion. Holford spoke of Christine;

he had lowered fatally, breaking only as far

as 'darling'. Her Holford wanted to kiss his

'darling' convulsively, to reach a bench

where women eating lunch listen to the secret voice

without so much garden. She she she. She

didn't think! She tried to collect in this way.

[...]

Jeff Keen seemed glad to see up. 'Dame,' he said,

and took Christine into an opening.

A healthy overlooking put whose

things *in* Christine? She ordered two coats and hats.

Since her feverish thinking, who was coming?

She found it impossible to chatter; no one else

was listening. 'Give me a hand. Over by the window!'

To start, easy going nonsense: 'Bubbles

can't stand work. Squeak was a pretty deary,

to give it my third language. What's your birth

certificate say? I prefer a fool. What do you want,

pleasing the girls? That fits you like laughter

finished a salesman.' Bubbles said, 'What a good sort.

Comes here. He's really loaded!' 'Celebrate your

everything in several bottles from a hat.'

What Corvell pulled out at random lengthily,

drunk for the time being, was for size natural. Christine

when she had 'how's that?' tasted her Babysham.

'Elle!

All right, you can get away with him! Christine,

tell me your secrets.' 'I've plenty on your friend,

but I'm *not* life.' Better honey was true generosity.

Christine, frowning, had come! Quickly

the room now punctuated those noises

so full of animal. Christine, her eyes towards

something uneasy, the beating of fear perhaps,

that sexual smile appeared to the room, which

Christine always regretted. Then intimate,

they revealed sex come, a timid blonde just now.

'You gay, you!' 'I came at thirst.' Bubbles went on

Christine, started to stay in this place with anything

forgotten, she had to, couldn't... She had forgotten

her free voice. She filled her reproach. 'Nice'

Corvell appeared. Christine, a very dark one.

He drew Christine undressing.

'The kid's a bit in her neck, disconcerted by cold.'

Girls delighted to drink the warmish over-sweet

liquid as if she were being acted by bare-shouldered

Holford. She saw handsome chilled condemned glass.

Christine was expected, was emptied. Frank jokes

kept her stoically saddled. Christine gripped her thighs.

Whispering fun was one establishment. Obscene

hand-fat softened her turn down. 'She's

in your place, in *my* place, "home".' Christine

was back in hope. 'He wants the bathroom.'

Her uneven firm breathing. Smile as you do,

Christine did, her breath came hard –

but showed her towards the door. 'It's no use,

you are hardly conscious!' She shivered thought,

so inflexible, so tough, it made one body. Christine

through amiable face-cruelty trembled, never could

suddenly fear; she recognised her dignity. Her line

of gratitude appeared in drink. Royston Ellis

(a wild one!) artistically arranged his task.

Christine pinched her outsides,

anything so revolting as slapping.

'You're going to like it. Take off Christine's

joking. You look twisted; you excite a fist

in his chest.' Full in her arms, he was stunned,

paying for bland features. His pleasure produced

transformation: Christine gripped his discoloured face

into a bit of fun. Too much sensuality made Christine

powerless to put her clothes back on! Ignoring

the degradation, the man who caused it fled. *She* fled

shining streets, her despair twisting through her brain.

Caterpillars could not think of finding everything

walking more. She would serve impossible space,

animal exhaustion hugging the shadows.

This time she surrendered to memories,

though she was mortally afraid of the day's

events in detail. She had just lived those memories

since her decision. Her memories

appeared in the night club concierge's looking up,

the entrance to her barmaid's variously reflecting

moments in front of her. All the mirrors

kissed by swollen lips ran back to Elle.

She flung herself towards the

blue lights of the scarlet Pontiac.

Her emergency was finally rising to suppress

her consciousness! The surface of Holford's

face held nothing. She wasn't worried as she

went into her body. She undressed her face

till it was all she could do. Murder in her dressing

gown froze with hair. A fire committed Holford

giving off an unmistakable Holford, 'I forgot she was smell!'

Friends were theatre-coming. Did she

remember early dinner relieved sweet midnight?

Holford so closely said, hesitantly, 'I'd really insist

I'm not caught out tonight. Nice people told me so.'

Cruel night: spiritual weariness she could not return.

She was nothing when he came. Monster Christine

jumped some special line, some hours went by.

She pretended to be approached through the sham.

The person in the idea was simply punished

when Holford groaned. Her mirror appeared

on her face. Her features were her bed.

Daylight came against her pillows

like discovery. Waking was one gloomy chaos.

Between terror and regret, neither shame

nor justice, the morning brought a clumsy

trick. Holford was a dim hope, but at least

she telephoned. Daylight seemed impossible

all morning, ceaselessly getting every minute

of engagement. Many booked after

to spend a moment alone with Christine.

Sudden frenzy. She gave out understanding:

he did not go home. Disarmed, Christine,

tired out, fell, following a dozen duties.

The day was imposed on her;

evening was exhausting her fears

and even her distance. The hectic rush

of unreality would not need to suffer

strong instincts. Christine now began

like a gambler – the danger was over cards.

[...]

His first dream of ritual he'd suddenly cured

softly, consumed by opium fumes.

Bubbles' smell worked strongly on quiver.

Jeff Keen was tempted, but not by first-fruits!

CHAPTER: JUST PAUSED TO CONSIDER A PARTNER

They'd never had a secret – secret pictures.

Secret Bubbles had a man. It's not like a man;

that woman listened carefully to the subject daily,

a semi-cloistered chance. Now she asked to leave

life! Words yield a clue I won't say. The very last

minute was proved right. A few minutes later,

Christine Holford spoke in the most glacial want.

The sweat must have cost her.

The ghastly effort wanted nothing more.

The bell cured her sordid thought dead – but corrupted.

A good client told her Squeak lacked

variety! An empty Peter Corvell hesitated

to have fitted Corvell together. Elle, so

educated! For a second, Squeak was paler

than her shoulder, Bubbles was stroking girls.

'Everyone here?' Voice realising anyone.

'Bubbles, when I leave somebody's mistress,

I can't let them know!' Lying, she was

ashamed of Elle, stretching luxuriously

towards the door. Corvell took her back.

'I'm not interested in a glimpse of a whole
begged body, not without a word for it!'
Expression, sent off to find her imprint
in soft mud, murmured, 'Please!' Corvell
pushed it from her. She said, 'Shut the door
like a good godmother,' as if private, sitting lucky.
'That's affection.' She said, 'Didn't you feel
Christine was *true*?' She gave the worktable
a movement to take off her permission.
'Smile familiar please. Come up! Waiting
in the cupboard goes without: you've got to have
violent resistance!' 'Plainly, every other day
I can't.' Begging her to come made Christine
tremble. The two girls quivered.

Half regretfully, we're used to
heated white teeth. She answered, 'Very
good,' with an ambiguous smile, 'won't you
catch Bubbles?' Christine put on all her
clothes, filled with silence. Bubbles removed
confusion to her senses. Hot vision: the sudden
professional indifference, all three firm, healthy.
Christine embarrassed an aristocratic rose.
Virginal feelings built Christine's shoulders,

better kissing, went pale. 'Bubbles' want will show

you your bell, Elle! Your dress was smaller

than the others'.' Black screen switched on

Jeff Keen. Toilet dark already, she went

straight to the men who had followed her.

Squeak's voice

was infinitely sad ... Christine

swung around without quite

knowing a fraction lighter. No

longer Squeak, we all

have our secrets. Christine's movement

didn't matter: 'My husband's an invalid.

I am boring. Talk

with the clients to explain.

They say I'm natural enough,

this wretched maladjustment puzzle.'

Who would give her the key to this place,

Christine inquired, then found out

she could just about go for what she wanted.

'I might, you know. I

saw a darkness that

was the red accent.' The savage

anger made her jump. Elle of Daylight

reigned into marks of night-face.

She sobbed imperiously. She pulled Squeak,

a little crazy too. 'I'm on my hands, come and

show Christine the scarlet Pontiac prostitution.

Bubbles does herself between teeth.' Her disgust:

passive Christine had been allotted degradation!

Royston Ellis's caresses found herself moved:

pleasure wages of her body faced the ordeal Christine

made, escaped her senseless feelings. Her terror

approached her house, plumbing perversion.

Inscrutable, insane, salvaging could do Christine.

She believed her external purification had no gift

for dissimulation. ('Take time: voice clumsily!')

Harvey Holford managed to behave normally until

Harvey Holford questioned her as a novice in sin.

Sheer animal movements shadowed

his senses: he was not the first step!

She: intuition; guilty haste.

The meal was going to do some coming.

She asked nervously when Holford had his study

and she swore to momentarily withdraw her book.

She had more attention that dawn. Memories

crushed her usual chair, alone. She realised

better than this bookish serious mind, misery

was so attentively fled. The book made no comment

but was about to stammer. Christine's husband

heard she went into reverse. 'Be alone, go to bed,'

he said with such authority. (Kiss his words!)

Christine would have welcomed her room.

The truth on her bed. Perhaps he bit

the pillow just to stifle a prayer, vast as time.

(Let me end this outburst.) Undress: the images

of two muddied Squeaks and Bubbles, for only

their promises were made in vain. She yielded enough

to appease fate. She refused her reason. She woke

limp leaves out of this heavy husband. Blowing

Holford, she became fully conscious of the horror

of speaking. A wife, damned like this, motionless,

she continued to play games. 'Listen about it,

the world is meaningless. I'm lying awake

in love with that thought.'

A queer followed by someone else!

'Laughter, protestations and you really love anyone else?'

Holford thought of love without distraction:

'Love my whole!' 'Can't I be unhappy?' Shining
with doubt seemed marvellously close to death.
Such humble wrong, suddenly Christine was without
an upheaval. She had been a fool on his face:
'You were Christine, *interrupted*.' 'I'll dissuade her
while he operates every waiting room. That time I'll meet you
dressed in a second decision.' He had Holford's
servant to her bed, beautifully transferred.
Her fondness roused physical hunger
that hardened Holford's face. Sleepless, lurking
in dubious desire, she would feel a pressing door,
if she made good the fear of running. Holford
accompanied Christine's true pleasure.

Jeff Keen made her period: 'Trollably
going sponsive every pected pleasant
sion of Corvell's interminable displeasure talked.'
Over-heated, she now listened to the girls' dim
lullaby to satisfy everyone's confirmed lovers.
Squeak had left her nice. She invented Bubbles'
conjectures, seduced her as a girl. She had
adored another man's mistress (she had!).
But she stuck to give a little time to Elle.
The house jumped at the chance of their desires.
[...]

Christine submitted to pleasure. Royston could not
revive such ludicrous study. It upset her. She
was the most intimate feel for her to shudder.
Tricks revolted her soiled love-humiliation.
Christine realised her sense of now. All
that remained was looked over. Others watched.

She could feel pride within, relish
submission when Christine remembered that
emptiness tormented Holford. It was *this* emptiness.
Christine: his exploded wife! Ease of the life
protecting and finding false existence:
'To be of not to be!' His fear began to
wonder about his nervous humour. Tenderness
of her local lack of private symptoms;
it seemed anxiety found no love for redoubled,
happier, remembered, disturbed night clubs,
the Calypso *and* the Blue Gardenia. Christine told him
about that discarded woman who could be kind.
Christine was sensual each morning. Holford
suffered Christine's face each morning:
he needed a submissive being! Christine herself
realised love was assuming she could not help depths
to which she had fallen. She developed qualities

that had once felt terribly old.

He became adoration for his cleanliness.

Racked by the hopeless situation, she

stepped over fact. She hated that place

in Queen's Road. She forgot her love for

suffering three times a week. Love now drove her

to lassitude and home. Christine every day increased

her returning agony. She escaped mental anguish.

Christine wondered whether there was enough

for her to give herself to the boatman, hold

her long depths. Martyrdom soiled Master Corvell

for her hat. Christine disappointed the bell,

and they were drunk. A market labourer around the room

on his knees she undressed with a word. His body

was in his eyes. Christine suddenly groaned

at her aspect, thicker than ordinary fury, desire slaking.

Satisfying this man whose undefinable flood

appeared on her face became relaxed. Her teeth,

happy and young, would have been amazed,

but she ignored them. The bedside duty she received

reached the end of her beginning.

Nothing else had the right race of joy, physical

joy, which had shuttered all her drives. Christine

seemed a disgusting conquered hell,

filled with an enormous strange animal.

Hard Christine did Squeak until that moment,

that evening. In surprise Elle was astonished

by Christine's quick radiant voice

that made no attempt to analyse. (She did not.)

'Reactivate her body striking again!'

She picked the flame and the bliss!

Christine escaped special circumstances.

She gave the answer to her afternoon.

A package on Master Corvell's doorstep

announced, pronounced, himself. It had

a charming voice, words of only one meaning.

Dozens disliked irony since it was spoken broad:

'Well-dressed gentle girls, suggest me that!'

(Similarly anonymous, I shut my fate.) 'Ugly Master,

my finger you see with a laugh.' Bubbles

kept at an exquisite madness, ruled.

Royston had the superior world. Such exploits

confused and touched him as pleasure-guessed.

Instead, Christine remained alone with her

disinterest. Squeak was nice to Squeak.

Something exclaimed, 'You're glad you aren't

vanity. I'm avaricious. I wouldn't make a little

cash in the form of the most expensive girls.

Affectionate ladies, do you really refuse

to drink to my first book?' The writer wondered what book

shopwindows unwrapped. He had put on the same title.

The last copy he inscribed 'Loving Dedication'.

He was moved by price tagged copy.

False Squeak's *his* Christine. He

could not resist. Eyes honoured with a jerk.

His pocket women brought in happiness.

The bell rang.

'I must go,' said Royston, brought into the life

of sudden silence. 'Christine's eyes glowed

with the joy of me,' Royston told the world.

Something passed to recall that request

of her world: *he* merely kissed *him*.

Christine would pick you, waiting. She had

a dismal memory impregnated with raw leather.

So avid, after lying quietly for the Master,

she went into Christine, heard her cultured resting.

[...]

She sat on hands still damp with body surroundings.

She knew Royston and his spiritual world

as men of the same class: she loved *charm*.

Jeff Keen was what he could not give: his taste,

his desire. All were poles beaten and flames

of this fatal life. Her flesh recognition was

her whole relief of insanity. She felt torture herself.

The dreadful twin melted again. Destiny refused

strangers to surrender a love. Other women

reproached her body, over the right of every

animal, the very cells of demanded spasm, suffering.

Christine existed like one moment only

to return, hardly realised. She was born!

She recovered her zest for life stronger

than ever; for now, she had, teeming

with monsters, to struggle to

maintain her path. Had Christine chosen

Holford, her doubts touching joy, she was

only by degrees servitude, daily:

Christine's time to feast drew

humility in this direction. Her husband was to obey

her too quickly, making him suspicious to give up

her balance. She could see her personality

alarmed him and she didn't want Master Corvell's goal. Christine was no longer able to recognise Holford's exorcised, separate, isolated life. Her body's secret flowers opened in virginal repose.

CHAPTER SEVEN (HARDLY NOTICED)

Vilasar Cresteef, Christine Holford, John Bloom,

met the sense of evil. 'Be nice to the face:

we got rid of him with a sigh all week.

You won't be sorry.' Who Squeak paid, her lover,

still had a hold, twice. Otherwise,

Squeak reached the Rough,

a barbaric hulk of true fat, taller than anyone cruel.

Christine pressed passionate then: 'Is he the creeps!?'

Elle (perhaps) the savage trap

(perhaps) licked them together. His

majestic dark fists slid slowly up her man.

Tiny Christine couldn't even say 'Veins!'

Fascinated, she couldn't take some bronze idol

to stare at these girls, but said, 'He didn't like

worrying!' It was intolerable but Bubbles

had to break Bloom. Gaiety did not answer,

'Take off your clothes, Squeak!' His shirt chest

showed some immense Bloom word. Her friend

was noticeably solemn, and that mattered.

The man's superb word seemed to be human,

magnetised by time. She saw a pair, but our attention

was still saying: 'Magnetised by Time.'

Christine started in a drawling voice. Squeak
stirred forbidden massive shoulders. Bloom
put his enormous seeming, so she was
surprised to relieve his attracted friend.
His companion bore the burden, this cynical fact.
(For more, I like that she had taken him
to her remark-senses, patient desire to whom
the immovable grease too tightly cut his ring.)
His clothes sparkled about his whole skin.
Christine remembered Bloom's grip. 'Narrow
shoulders have a keen emotion I like!' She pressed
his mouth against the bed. Her lips calculated herself.

The young man Vilasar enquired, 'What's Elle?'
his thin legs invading her cigarette case.
'Indifference or something? What's your
pleasure at secrets?' *Intimacy* also
was his dubious nickname on the pillow,
his cynical face sometimes not going to
realise the gums. One blow did not finish
that mouth! The bush managed to keep
forward, made of gold. Christine had frightened him,

rapidly going, 'I've got a friend short with going!'
Christine was Elle!

With his body, time was not for Bloom.
An animal's inside of thought, banished
from this watchful torpor, he stopped her
with a 'Wait!' Instant harsh gesture. 'You
are my fault!' he could explain himself
roughly. The first questions he no longer
tried to heat to forget the taste of a long time.
He kissed her gold jaw. She was never Elle!
Vilasar seemed to want to slake Christine; she
had to resist the twilight. Too contented to stroke Vilasar,
she could repress her hand, a sort of
gap in his buttonholes. He
was covered with belly, but the police record
of his voice acted on him like goodnight.

(Watch him dress, his scars virile and
mysterious.) Vilasar missed her
by her constant spread, languor wanting to pay
after a week in an evil grimace.
She was worried in staying away for welcome.
She suggested, 'I could, with insolent pride!'
[...]

He tossed! He came quicker! Christine whispered,

'Why haven't you come?' 'I didn't come,' he retorted

(that's talk in his voice), a seduction deeper

into Christine's image. Fidgety, trying to,

he sank harder to the ramparts, which crumbled!

She remembered that she had some friends,

by now burning from Vilasar's going. This breach

had one particular infatuation: Vilasar lost all sense

of Harvey Holford. Worrying about her kisses,

she dressed very slowly, broken to accept,

in order to 'turn' Holford, expected

at the night club in any case,

a fitting rushing home after transition.

An informal Christine went without her girls,

and she felt a little eye. Men rose intense, asked

by two surgeons. The darker 'Don Juan', he

moved on his face, sensuality tender and

tough. Attractive Christine! she felt ironically

this friend. He treated her some.

He held her audacity features for bluntness.

Far from an involuntary reputation, pathetic

Elle, his ardour appeared daily!

'Casanova' would never attain scars

in his pocket, the efforts of matter, no natural

savagery of love at that moment with the

golden mouth for her dance-partner.

Prescience cut out that evening (with the Angel

around her, she had one, I'm afraid). Bloom

refused to leave her. By her dress, by her skin,

he had Christine in perverse intoxication! Two

women kissed Holford with a start. Something heavy

was horrified. Thoughtlessness had hurt her love

for those moments she recognised in search

of her secret walls into her other world,

and she knew that the corrupt flood had fallen

into this dangerous situation: she risked losing

the dike. She looked forward in the darkness.

She said anything about the man

in her house. 'I don't see him

anywhere. You're sick.' When Christine left

it was before she made that body walk, paralysed

Jeff Keen. What she represented with a man

from the most vivid passion, her two worlds

separate, life in the shape of the trembling

terror situation she could bend to. She had

control, self-preservation ran towards a passing stumble.

A convict weight raised his voice to go somewhere.

His first step drained all her hurry, looking at a workman.

He did the *idea*, turning towards this word.

Downing such relish till his drink said, 'You

want to know how I keep out of trouble?

In The Blue Gardenia Club I tell you

his expression: you sent this shiver through Vilasar

and reflected an *idea*.' He went on, 'Vilasar's a boy!

Understand?' 'He has one weakness – me!

He asked his skin in the beginning. The man

can't see himself. Playing the fool, he let himself go.'

'You'd work up deep *thought*: think!'

She hadn't, and she wouldn't! 'I mean your shoulder.

Quick! It's making a huge empty glass!'

Fascinated, her maddened nerves told him: 'Shadow

slumped free again.'

She would be completely two

scared men, that pair she did, behind them,

obeying them. Jeff Keen told his friend

a total break with the Master. 'Yes lady.'

'Yes Master Corvell.' The interview

escaped Christine as her tormentors

between herself and Holford liked to take

their holidays. Hesitation with Bloom felt Jeff Keen.

'Herself' was coming on the clinic. Christine

knew him over, tender Holford alone in Brighton.

Haunted by love, her most wretched writhings

she had foreseen: Holford *and* Holford! Christine

was worried about his work, the evil gold and

the monstrous shadow of his worries. Wonderful

Holford shone, pristine pleasure as fresh as Christine.

Days:

quiet into eternity

were indeed lived through, stretching

her life with a

threat for happiness

so long. Her essence was like a delicate body.

She proceeded to sunlight; the sky

was a precious balm. The air bathed her body,

the touch of many chastely beloved young fullnesses.

He loved all she adored, his whole joy in the hired

schoolboys. Christine felt truly close to learned articles,

his books! Holford came between them;

vigorous innocent exercise served to unite them.

She was contentment. She pitied

total harmony after some hurt, risking the system.

So it was with resurrected love, to think of the

sting that disgusted. She shadowed the house.

She held her edge of self-assured distance.

Bloom would know where to find her hands.

They lay under Holford, protected by her own

weapons too rapidly. Royston Ellis haunted her,

realistic hippo-wrestler, as the pimp turned

into a sort of inarticulate safe. 'Poor kid himself,'

Christine thought, as mystical terror fell in

her carnal depths. The enemy thought everything

that drove her; the powers remained indefinitely

sweet, sad weather, crouching with life.

One morning it rained. Holford and Christine

revised an article on illustrated magazines.

She picked up Ellis. They had lain a couple

and were equally boring. Since she glanced,

the stories turned to a sequence of lines, then

the letters turned daily. She could understand Jeff Keen.

Then she remembered 'Jeff Keen'

was a nickname – he was working

sea and sky, clearing up the beach, mowing

the grass. She had given her left behind.

Studiously then, growing brighter, she said,

'It's a run on that greasy paragraph!' Zine

scrutinised the Blue Gardenia.

Holford was the call of the bed. Cry

the printed name, her debased filthy language,

euphemisms dirtier for their specialties.

Christine's mouth filled with a shameful,

bountiful heat. She calculated it was Holford;

she immediately had *not* been voiced.

Jeff Keen swam quickly, getting information.

The door slammed, trembling with fury built up

almost inaudibly. 'So, you're caught. Too bad

I'd retreated to explain something!'

Christine swung in the air, never

knew where to dodge the cut and his savage

energy. An idiot lash whistled

to find her agility. His belt held Vilasar

back: 'Your friends separated, filled the silence.'

They stayed, panting and gradually hauled her

into the squalid welt. Christine's face needed it,

Holford pictured this no longer. Her willpower
was saying, 'The others made him look up to the bed.
I don't care!' Christine had fallen semiconscious.
He muttered, 'There was something deeper of that
fallen angel, his usual imperceptible hurting
she enjoyed!' When he took her muscles
he wanted love making less than decrease.
Their union was flight.

Mysterious circles in imagination
were amenable to the idea of the underworld.
Strange thing – and linked to her!
Night Club Victim of Fatal Sharpness! Pleasure seeking
to stimulate her desire for imagining his young
life, her drives had dangerously moved.
She hoped herself at the core of her sensual evening.
It gave her the impossible. Imagine
how, watching for those secrets, it took Holford
out of waiting. For twenty-four hours
Vilasar and Bloom were near Hassocks.
Christine was in the bar as usual, but tonight was *lacking*.
Vilasar knew men: Bloom was a woman! Vilasar:
a whole evening going away. Bloom made him
quite foreign to his thing – he recognised a behaviour.

Who was rolled to eat a sign he was equally

pleased with? 'To Hell, Corvell, with the wisdom

of his unfathomable thought!' Hungry Christine: Elle

unbounded. 'Bloom, are we going to eat?' Vilasar

suggested Christine. Bloom added, 'That's

OK.' Vilasar bore enough swank

over the other two. Bloom accepted,

but not without animal awareness.

Vilasar intercepted Elle alone,

with a note of pleading: 'Get rough!

I'm singled out, as in a bad leading market!'

Christine accompanied God. Christine

thought existences. Vilasar

had been Bloom's padding will-power,

everyone ignorant of that, since they *must* spend.

The man behind his eyes round

the door of garlic, came freshly, 'Elle

will be pleased to see a woollen cardigan

greeting a skirt and blouse. You should be

vigorous coming!' The two men, touchingly

warm, looked her over. Christine smiled

fine black eyes, huge, despite her fat sweetheart.

'Her face,' said Elle. 'Minute!' declared Bloom

gravely. 'Let me do the indicated Maurice!'

he pronounced maternally.

Stuffed Maurice treated them

almost tenderly, a strong virile Maurice!

Bloom drew Christine into the room. They shook

her; she did not stop at the table. (Escorts differ.)

Heads revolved about the rich heavy heady wines,

idle eyes elusively stuffy. Spiced by Elle,

Bloom liked to curve Christine, the ponderous

shoulders feeling to look around. The bend

of clandestine Vilasar (being 'free' was

Vilasar's expression-effect), she used

some powerful potion on her women.

She asked herself with a tide of images.

Luridly sensual, Bloom whispered,

'I can't...' 'Guts!' he said to Vilasar.

Bloom's touch and her terror led them

to The Calypso Club, a strange contagion

above the Whisky a Go-Go, opposite

the low rubbish, the soiled empty room

and a queer breath drawn by gleaming

boots, big whips and cheap brandy. Barbaric

Vilasar settled the outside world when

she saw her sole protection between his teeth.

Bloom's pocked face cast a quick girl,

a seedy individual with Christine-talk.

Bloom was a dull void; Christine understood.

She flew to his coat pocket and dragged fingers at his belly.

'The man might fire Bloom's gaze,' said

the pocked man. His eyes got a small package

from the latter. 'You hypnotised his other

pocket and the weight.' Vilasar wouldn't shoot Bloom.

'We'll settle that man's Elle.' No coward

was whirling more beautiful as she

recognised his courage, to unleash death

just like *she* did. He saw the first guy follow.

'You go to bed, Christine – do you want

the faintest idea?' Tight kids, once alone

with Vilasar, wanted to give her cocaine!

Christine marked him. She felt The

Blue Gardenia suitable for her

excesses, to feel her burning desire.

Vilasar in the sordid little room

had scarcely begun. 'Dirty unutterable

joy!' Christine said, threateningly,

'I have Vilasar joking.' His usual self
grabbed his belt. Christine had
invincible power. No, that
unbearable look of Christine
could see spellbound Bloom, fighting
for life as long as the street. She swore
he was safe in bed. The pockmarked man
came back a few hours later, his face drawn
with begged appearance. Alone, Christine
without him for several days. Christine did come:
she had the feeling! 'Tell me why
I like honour!' Jeff Keen, going out tonight,
refused, quite harmless, almost gentle.

Christine was OK, he thought. She
answered him, and he left.
Following Bloom
and 'Blanche' (a young man),
the whole story got in the address.
Bloom and the real name of Elle
turned to Vilasar. He had *known*,
being in the world. The fight he was
preparing for Bloom would have
murdered his pallid mouth.

CHAPTER EIGHT

Out of kindness, he

had no control of

his weapon. More complex,

Vilasar Cresteef,

at first, *made* Christine

Holford at about four o'clock:

each detail summoned a rich gentleman.

Christine's memory instructed them.

Christine's quiet grace went into the big room.

The man was a glimpse of second. His bony

figure would have opened somewhere.

To run away, Peter Corvell would never

have made that movement. Her new drained step

told on her. Jeff Keen found her unable to grow;

John Bloom felt trapped: the small moment,

human power, beside the fleeting afternoon.

'Sit down!' giggled Bubbles. '*Christine!*'

She slipped into a deadly grip!

'Refreshment, ladies? If you would care

for whoever names Elle, Elle of her voice!'

Bloom's disconcerting charm hung loosely

against her body, hands stuffed with his

moment. Drinks were courteously declined.

His presence began to discuss studied care,

phrases that tore up Christine's fear. Trifles

pointed piece by piece: horrible Bloom laughed!

He flickered with horror to feed and increase

the pursuit of that divinity. Christine denoted

lust, ambiguous retorts, this ambivalent game.

Bloom paid for the mantlepiece, and leaning,

said, 'Farewell prostration!' Christine

watched a desperate certain Corvell in Elle.

Soon she had Bloom go, probably

to his more morbid pleasures.

Christine stammered, protested,

stretching her arm out to Corvell,

to think. 'Now, now! what is monsieur silent

for?' 'The triumph to be waiting for

Elle!' 'Take monsieur to your usual

customs!' 'Me?' added Bloom, with a

slightly unsteady behind. Hysteria

cried out, 'Christine dared you by

chance! Why answer?' 'I'll scream, throw

myself out of the disgust!' 'Stay, human

being.' 'Disgusted Bloom

wanted to see my bed! Do you want

dirty photographs, because his delight

became too obvious for a moment?' Then

seeing that Christine took her hand off

his thin cold fingers, an enormous melancholy

waited, remained silent, he with the tips.

Christine was haggard. 'Just me, better than you?'

Quietly, she fell back on the scarlet coverlet,

schoolgirl resurgence of desire. Bloom felt

exhausted: his pleasure kept him hunched forward.

He rose, frightened. The only minute

her impassioned agony pulled up the movement

of her coverlet over the bed, a hand's promise.

Even in his most depraved moments,

Holford wouldn't ever know the idea in Bloom's

head, fateful seconds prolonging the voluptuous agony

afforded him. He could not thrill

at the sight of Christine's broken expression.

He could not maintain the pose. Venomous

Christine heard Master Corvell going away.

She got up like a lunatic. 'You must forget –

you don't know who I am!'

CHAPTER 9: THE HOURS CAN HARDLY BE DESCRIBED

Harvey Holford was impatient
and John Bloom, on leaving Master Corvell,
suddenly remembered sporting, that Bloom
and Holford had the slightest racing through facts.
Christine Holford's head had no doubt. Martyrdom
would have restrained her little moral principles.
What moral in any case stood for her perversity?
Demon Bloom alone described the bitter debauch,
not with remorse. His double was bound to talk.

A universe of goblins moaned feebly
like Christine. Punishment committed her sense of hell,
a semi-injustice of her fate anticipating
shadows. Lost in the dark love, she felt Holford's
coming. She heard him doing reverberated
walks. Her system: taking off his hat. Mirror only
trying to control now, Christine held her moment,
fatally certain, every Bloom of their feelers
through the doorknob. Their rust deliverance
actually rushed into her. Christine experienced then
the tortures of water. Holford smiled at tomorrow,
Holford flooding into her eyes; Holford

was surely happy breathing. They spent the night
(carefully).

'Bend over, you find out love for you!'
That fine love for Christine murmured his little
'Why not?' 'Don't be a pillow for the human condition!'
She wept irreconcilably.
The small details at each memory repeated,
an incantation; thought brushed the words,
'Don't be reminiscences of dawn, prayers
after first light!' Christine had *all* hope for innocent
revealing. Imagine some sign, then someone else:
terror would be everything. One word
to Bloom would resist pleasure, like the night.
She had visited Holford for lunch.
She asked, 'Each second beating drop?'

Bloom haunted her mind, which
grew to the point at which insanity
mustn't leave her. Christine's heart
might have learnt the truth from his return;
Holford she loved, fadedly. Cerebral matter
could not go away. Her best Bloom would
still an agony even more. Eating a storm cloud,

her vision blurred. Chosen by Bloom, even

tightening at her throat, imminent adversary

depressed; she struggled against her husband,

'You can't leave a sick child to notice the burn!'

Christine gave knowledge of safety,

and her wretched heart answered the calls she could not

stand. Fearfully, Holford was going to faint!

To calm herself, she answered her shoulders.

They slept together,

Christine now lax a little

by actually touching the man.

'Give up breathing!'

A longer little discovery

could not hold for a second.

She knew the city where

they would meet fear.

He certainly went limp.

She ought to use Bloom,

the worst possible terror.

She wouldn't play

her barmaid's silence. She

was not total. Christine

clung to Holford. Bloom

called his own motive 'infamy',

her husband hung up as an effect

of her humiliation.

On her knees, the barmaid came!

Christine wouldn't give his gold teeth

under any other circumstances (she was Bloom's

else). Vilasar Cresteef, in her presence,

was full of anything natural. Christine surprised,

her totally indifferent reactions:

Vilasar, predictable; Harvey,

preventable; Bloom, who lusted after her ...

Vilasar cut short her unconcern. Christine gave him

mounting style: he'd prepared discomfort

between fading anger; he had general inferiority

in the same vague want. He loved her

thought-matter. 'Aren't you surprised how

I gesture, *Elle*, dangerous body? You mustn't say

"sincerity forgotten!"' His voice added:

'Don't blackmail yourself.'

Fond surprise! Half-crazy, he came into

the squeezed Daydream. Christine shook her future –

frightened shoulders felt she was not to shake her out.

[...]

'My husband's married!' A photograph caught
all her youth. She had looked: Vilasar's vital,
impossible come. 'I can help nobody.'
He made her repeat another night,
feverishly, soon enough, too frantic for The
Blue Gardenia. He made her repeat another.
An automaton whirlpool from its narrowest
centre of the vortex, first flung, she felt
herself. He made her repeat.

They formed masks, the
faces of sleepless nights. Cardboard
Holford had reached such a longed-for bed.
Christine prayed, half aloud, 'I must take
you out of the neighbourhood!
I'm going at 12:30. Madame Holford wrote
this today.' Christine's voice rose to a bind;
she recognised her wishes with men. Resignation
lasted until the silence of death. She began to
pace her madness on her knees! 'I'm Holford,'
(he'll tell every Vilasar).

When reason repeated over
and over, she entered his first

movement. She barely dressed,

a dubious draw: fate cut him! She asked,

'Won't we get to Palace Pier as

a damp towel? I don't know if you

asked to connect two ideas.' Christine's temples

wrong with feeling, her hypnotic matter.

Vilasar did not even *feel,* Christine blindly

seeking his protection. Everything conspired

to dampen his love for her underworld.

Vilasar shall be late

at the place. 'An hour'll

show you, she would calm

down, her whole being,' he said,

'*plunged*!' He rejoined the

scarlet Pontiac in the side street, a whispered

protest: 'Teach me

in overalls! I'm a battered

shirt!' A few minutes later, a ready

jacket dropped them inside the courtyard

of The Royal Pavilion. Little

Albert and Bloom

went into the garden. She glanced

at Master Corvell's 'house'. 'My husband's

everything, because he couldn't
have you!' The bastard, in a
cold unnatural tone talking, could
have been 'fixed' there and then.

She had come! Touched by the
straight worry she said, 'I'll fix
a clump of trees in front of the library.'
They sat there afterwards. 'Afterwards?
You'll be resolutely another word!'
This man had time to bench the distance,
pointed him out to
Christine: Christine felt so good!
On Kings Road, the Pontiac, whose strength
never felt less, stood up. Bloom
was leading to the mistake. Little Vilasar asked,
'Show courage?' He ordered Christine's sign.
She didn't move the Pavilion. She saw
the Dome under the garden. 'Holford
entered my husband!' She, releasing
a killer dog, was sinister!

Christine started to run Vilasar through the gate.
Instinctively, mindlessly, Vilasar had entered

his Pontiac Parisienne. 'Albert, get in,' he said;

they listened, all rushing.

Contemptuously mingled cries waited.

A police sergeant ran to the spot.

Albert trod Holford. (Bloom wrote

that he would telephone conquest of her. She proposed

to give up a shameful morning. Tiresome,

without a word, she was the

plausible silence. Naturally,

Holford filled him with reason, Christine's

danger like eaten evil genius. Noble Bloom

sought to fight intensely, since he should keep these

conflicts arranged.) The promenade

went straight towards little Holford.

Christine's murderous vehemence

stiffened men like battle. 'Hold him back!'

Agility

on Holford's uneasiness went to meet his

violent motion. He ran his pocket for that plot of guesses.

Switch-goes Albert will be on his own,

upskilled on his intended rushing.

Holford saw a warning.

Bloom drew back his instinct-front.

[...]

There was Vilasar, but Holford had a metal snarl.

His knife saw a contracted face.

Holford might have got away, holding

the fleshless body. Police whistles lay quite still.

TEN DETOURS

Under

the Clock Tower, he told Christine

Holford she did not understand:

'Watch the Pontiac, it's obvious.'

Picked up, Christine obeyed passively.

Vilasar Cresteef glared at her;

he merely growled! She spoke

in good papers, a woman talking out of

her stupor stopping the moment. The Pontiac

disappeared swiftly. Christine seemed

the aimless imagined vehicle, the

jolting car she was driving for silent

Little Albert. Between herself

and no living creature could groping painfully forward-link the fact

to decipher the meaning of men and of herself:

her chaotic soul lay ahead. Abstract symbols

had beaten John Bloom. Innumerable stops killed him.

Bloom would not see Harvey

Holford again; the cause of no

more, in fact, he left to be surprised

on her bed. Back home, Christine
had Holford immediately. She lay down
ringing to wake her barmaid. Madam
Christine opened something terrible.
'There's a doctor to tell you about sleep.'
Her first thought before dying, she said,
was so insistent: suddenly from Holford's
milk bar, The Whisky a Go-Go, an incredible
accident! Christine's rigidity – nothing critical –
was stabbed so violently you
must be mistaken. 'Sadly, we have all already been
arrested. That man, your husband, recovered chance.'

So many suffering bodies in the care of men
waited for memory. No more recognised,
her first visit confirmed her circle as total.
Jeff Keen of unreality and protective times
called him his 'world intonation'. The professor
was really there, cut short! Christine's hands
retained a blunt dear anything.
He said, 'I'll... I'll know... I'll know better...
Don't answer for Holford's life tomorrow!'
Christine had accepted herself, bandaged.
The face more than asleep made Christine

a sort of ghastly 'herself'. The middle of waxy,

motionless, flaccid pity, though lifeless: eyelids fallen.

The firm flesh, bountiful youth,

could not tell what threatened her animal

instinct. Only that morning, Holford,

for good health, had armed anything!

Her brutal lover dreamed of

whispered waiting, a painful inquiry.

'Madam Holford, your husband

is still unable against the wall!' Christine

thought: 'Her barman hustle has told you

dizzied arrest, doctor.' Holford took

the detective to one job, added quietly,

'Give the poor woman a very hard ride.'

They watched the policeman realise she was free.

The barman penetrated her! She bit her

understanding, sharpened. 'Bloom

told you,' she recollected, 'he'd given

consciousness a "terrifying clarity-leap"!'

Only the Pontiac led her to the source.

'I'll show you,' the professor said,

'He's a shock of that nature, doesn't quite

promise assurance.' What did it matter

the rest of the time? Motionless with terror,

then, reassured, she tried strange relaxation

of getting dark. Would his heart ask her

what came to change the wound? That *dark* wound

in all the world knew she undressed Vilasar!

His revolver under Christine held her,

released home! Her hand chattered much.

'The professor'll answer for tomorrow. We'll see

a kind of inner secret – irresistible – recognised.'

She thought her whole story directly;

she was expecting 'yes'. Bloom's 'presence'

she saw absently. (Strange company

can listen to fire and flames.)

Christine filled the moment, staring

in front of the melt. 'A flutter of her loved me!'

Something worse in Christine's answer:

'I supposed an emotion he couldn't understand.'

'Christine set the best side of me.' If only

he'd watched Holford, that knife of his! What

passion shuddered, with a sadness that murmured

something noble. Closely, the people motivated by death.

In the name of little experiments, he

continued thoughtfully. *Vice versa*

when he first caught vague thoughts:

'How well is anyone who needs you more

than Christine?' Vilasar corrected himself,

drew his attention. He reminded tomorrow

of the professor's poor broken sanity.

Innocently stretched out on a red sunny morning, he

was now wretched, pleading with the fact.

Could Elle gesture?

Who had perversely pierced Holford's mystery?

Tenderly he touched her softest blanket over

the morning of recuperation. Purely physical, she

regretted her only agony had visited Bloom. Holford

was everything, hopelessly miserable.

Their conversation the night before

felt awkward; *neurotic* seemed to make sense.

His shadows had fled gestures of the great

fatal symptoms, had slept another step and,

thereby being changed, prompted no more than danger.

Hypersensitivity to life heard she had not been bad.

Her tormented journey would take him in the shade.

Once again: great trees, smooth snow. Holford's eyes

at least lacked all that fate loved. A dying man did not

recognise her flinch-depths. Dreadful, she bent over

a quiver in the trembling flame.

She moaned, 'No, don't!'

The doctor said, 'All right. What's wrong

with the most learned plane

of your controlling husband's numbed features?

Penetrate its frightful bed passionately

on the pillow as slack as Holford's stare.'

He was absurd. Surprised by her cries, she said,

'Your boss could not prevent herself!' Holford,

the smallest superhuman, rose.

The constant flicker deluded her: Holford's Holford

wanted his flesh. Christine bent over a deep

and loving reply in the corridor.

She talked to their waver-room:

'Was she a sound coward too, *darling*?'

Suddenly Christine remembered something

worse in the war, total recovery from a dull medical word;

'Paralysis! Paralysis!' she repeated.

As long as she had not known, immobility belonged.

An anonymous truth advice: 'Make him difficult!

[...]

Numb his sickness savagely!' 'With others,

I don't want to,' Christine interrupted Holford.

Absolute determination in Christine's face

– that fighter! Day glowed like lost lanterns.

Her own life was closed within the close,

a body powerless to transmit matchless victory,

she thought. Holford's lips trembled.

His forehead was able to form syllables.

Folds in Christine's soul would

come about at the end of the week. Fingers

pulled through complete attitude. She had rung up

his wound for the rest. His body – his arms and torso –

satisfied Christine. Holford had begun

two experiments: he could read Christine,

crippled, bringing home joy to formulate spasmodic

everything. Holford's lips hated to move back in.

His books, being incomplete, Christine felt everything.

She had to nurse Holford back to a barmaid: 'Madam,

I didn't want the papers! Christine! If you'd

seen the pictures of Christine!!'

(The murderer heard nothing.)

All seemed up and

down, to sit down. Vaguely

gold teeth swayed rhythmically, herself

swaying with them, talking to

Christine, sorry the outside

world … anyone must tell the police!

Tentacles entangling her ransom,

the barmaid asked Christine the results of her

interrogation. She'd be complexity

of his fleshy coffin made

absurd. The barmaid looked

down a little (of course): 'Testimony

won't lose the moment, but I feel badly

for sensation.' A hunted animal filled

Christine at bay. Society had trained Holford to sleep.

Death entered the icy deliverer.

Holford's struggle murmured and asked him to come!

A furious end telephoned his accomplice.

'It's worse than reading the papers. The police

are conspicuous. Your Vilasar

went to the person-photographs. It was Jeff Keen

the other two recognised.' In short, a girl

in the policeman in a

car at the moment noticed the Pontiac.

[…]

'The papers attack aliases!' 'There
isn't a paper!' Elle said, 'Christine, what spite?'

Moral theories are the law, giving
up all thought. Mistaken Elle said, 'Who
admired my love of imprisonment?'
Elle left no trace of foreseeable chance,
breathed a single last lying. 'Please
point at common sense, keep
hold of credited others.' Christine
started to list their wind, some dread clamour
of conducting Holford. She grinned suddenly,
mouth filled with gold talk.

To see Holford, Christine called in her advised girl.
'I wouldn't have released Christine's tremble!'
She begged to postpone the barmaid
a week immediately prior to the suffering.
She'd heard talk of rising degradation,
a boundless proverb:
A foreign God is capable into Infinity. Her martyrdom
brought her a smile and wonderful discoveries.
Holford, tarnishing his love with the knife
of a lover, had a faultless body.
[...]

All his strength picked up in the Pontiac,

Holford had to defend courage

to go back to Vilasar. Jeff Keen entangled the surface.

Sunk those leaden days,

she had to appear

calm and had to be her

presence: a 'thing' she was.

Drugs felt the need to

think of contented *him*.

Asked for that lost face

in the next room

to read the information

about everything,

the enigma of reporters,

the clothes Elle described,

the Holfords' young

man, Jeff Keen

discussed doorbells,

imagined the report.

Harvey Holford's husband

was not *Professor* Holford.

From the pelvis down,

wild convulsive laughter.

[...]

'Possibly the neck and arm

muscles dead, doctor.'

The Professor asked to see the papers;

the papers' fearful

hesitation had words, I'm afraid.

Elle, a sick woman, so pointlessly stabbed. He

could not read that name: his expressive tortured

photo-time. Christine, full of her notorious 'freedom',

would have her Friday. She knew the district

and today was Sunday. She had a funny picking,

grey lips contracted immediately in a dead voice.

'Darling', forming, wandered the pages of attention.

His cheeks quivered slightly, but these creased

signs convinced her, a hired boat to kill her.

In the bar of the Blue Gardenia,

among a dozen others, Vilasar

continued, 'And that was all

right! Keep calm!' The two men, crazy,

ground his jaws. He's that hard!

He stared grimly at the day after tomorrow.

'You under-moaned a minute, followed

a profound surprise.' They accepted neutrality

in the heat of Bloom as a friend played out, *finally*.

Christine looked him in the world!
'My husband I love more to touch Bloom
half done for! I used to worry about your
cripple! I took the bit of weeks.' Her words
robbed her voice of the slightest sensation of fact.
Gaining filled her with a nameless runner.
'Bloom's morning once scooped a shapeless
everything.' She made no reply. Vilasar
missed the landing stage
for Vilasar! He was *coming!*

She switched on her legs, and then
wrung her trembling shame: shame-eyes!
'Always to be so dearly happy!' she stammered,
shaking her head beside the twisted Pontiac,
'No more!' She knew not to die, to free her
like a chest struggle. She knew no salvation.
She longed for pressing hands
to ensure her motive, false virtue to confess spite.

Three years, a human
heart

trembling,

fearful experiences, now

gone. Three years

by the sea.

2022-23

AFTERWORD: SHARP GAS LIPS UNDER HER FLESH SUDDENLY WHITE IN THE HALLWAY

Watching the early films of Jeff Keen, I noted the repeated appearance of what I thought of as 'the pink auto'; I had read somewhere that this colourful Pontiac Parisienne belonged to a nightclub owner in Brighton. Keen continued to use footage of this automobile throughout the 1960s, though I think he only borrowed its gangsterish gleam for an afternoon's shoot, to make the 11-minute black and white silent 8 mm film *Breakout* (1962). The incongruity of seeing this mammoth American car on film squeezing past the familiar Clock Tower in Brighton (my local city as I remember it vaguely from the early 1960s) was most impressive, if uncanny. A heritage that one hadn't inherited. A city that wasn't yet a city. It was not until I read Richard Davenport Hines' *An English Affair* (2013), about the nefarious goings-on of cabinet minister John Profumo, that I linked the car, which was mentioned in passing, and the films of Jeff Keen with a precursor scandal of the Profumo debacle, and its Brighton setting. It was a sordid story concerning a Conservative MP and washing machine importer, John Bloom, and Christine Holford, the wife of the nightclub and Pontiac owner. The result was that, in 1963, a jealous and taunted Harvey Holford murdered Christine Holford, spitefully shooting her in the genitals. The subsequent trial and the minimal sentence Holford received, before an all-male jury, leaves a bad taste in any aesthetic appetite that desires to utilise this material (as does his candidacy for a far-right party under his new name in the 1974 General Election). Books and DVDs gathered dust on top of my filing cabinet, as I recoiled from contaminating this material or being contaminated by it. I knew, as Iain Sinclair says somewhere, that the guilty ones are the writers, who disinter pain again and again without compunction. I waited some years, hoped for some sympathetic magic, appropriate forms.

I *did* want to utilise this material and I *did* want to make the link to the extraordinary films made by Jeff Keen, who I met on a couple of occasions, even visiting his Brighton flat with Lee Harwood; I remember a column – no other word for it, it reached the high ceiling – of Marvel comics, which he used as raw material in his later *Blatz!* movies. I felt that *my* raw material would have to include Keen's work, the car, its murderous owner, his victim wife, as well as two favourite and iconic films of the era, Michael Powell's *Peeping Tom* (1960) (that subsequently disappeared from the project, despite my discovery that its script was written by an ex-Bletchley code-breaker who used to send encryptions as *poems*!), and Luis Buñuel's *Belle de Jour* (1967). Notably, this surrealist masterpiece of the sixties is based upon realist pulp from 1928: Buñuel hated Joseph Kessel's moralistic and misogynist novel of that title, in which a woman is condemned for her secret sexual desires (as was Christine Holford with her more public affairs and flirtations). The film is not a parody or pastiche of its model; it's perversely faithful to its twisted but conventional morality. The novel was perfect material for post-surrealist transformation. In 1969, an English translation by Geoffrey Wagner from 1962 was rushed into a second paperback edition with a picture of a simpering Catherine Deneuve on the cover, a 75p charity shop purchase.

Uncertain how I would approach and proceed with these materials, I decided to work on my copy of the novel with an analogous disrespect to that shown by Buñuel: I treated *Belle de Jour* using the technique I have always called 'Tom Phillipsing', finding new linguistic content in this old novel, as Phillips had with *A Human*

Monument, as he transformed it into the bubble texts of *The Humument* (ignoring for a moment the brilliant visual side of the work!). There is something of gentle gathering, enclosing, about the method, which is absent from the tearing violations of the superficially similar cut-up technique. Both are versions of collage, or montage, of course. So Mayer expresses what I have thought for a long time, possibly half-consciously: 'Montage arouses us; while plenty of attention has been given to its ability to awake us critically to rise up, the role of its erotic charge in calling us to action has been ignored, unseen and unwanted.' (*A Nazi Word for a Nazi Thing*, 2020)

At some point during this slow process (one page Tom Phillipsed a day, 140 pages), I watched Daniel Farson's ATV television programme *Living for Kicks* (1960) which partly took as its focus the teenage clientele of the Whiskey a Go-Go milk bar (such pre-*Clockwork Orange* innocence!) near The Clock Tower in Brighton. I already knew that this establishment was part of the entertainment complex run by Harvey Holford: upstairs lay the more exclusive Blue Gardenia and Calypso clubs (where alcohol was served). Farson's documentary – the old Soho soak feigns shock at teenagers snogging and disdaining marriage – features an intelligent and knowing interview with a proto-Beat poet called Royston Ellis, whose name was familiar to me, but *not* from my knowledge of underground poetry of the 1960s, which I'd foolishly thought comprehensive. In fact, the name was floating before me in Ye Cracke pub where, after lockdown, I regularly met a group of Liverpool friends (the informal 1955 Committee). On the mirror under which we often sat is an engraved commemoration of a joint poetry-music gig by Royston Ellis and John Lennon in Liverpool in 1960. (Ellis called his performance poetry 'rocketry' and he had already performed with The

Shadows. Ellis, who died in 2023, needs incorporating into that history of the underground.)

One afternoon, I suddenly noticed the memorial to this performance. Something was happening here, I felt, to speed this project along; I conceived of superimposing the shadowy Brighton reality upon my distorted version of Buñuel's *Ur*-text. Both narratives involve a jealous murderer. I replaced Kessel's names, Buñuel's *dramatis personae*, with the names of the participants in the Brighton tragedy: acquaintances and lovers of the fatal couple (Thatcher, Hatcher, Bloom, Cresteef), and employees and habitués of the night clubs (Corvell, Bubbles and Squeak), with the addition of the artist figures Jeff Keen and Royston Ellis, and a few necessary others. 'Elle' was the Tom Phillipsed 'Belle' persona of Kessel's anti-heroine, the titular haunting (but *who* is 'she' in this reworking?). I transposed place names from Paris to Brighton without irony. (Virène was a character entirely derived from a place name and he becomes my 'Jeff Keen'!) The text passed through many stages of transformation ('states' an engraver might have called them) both mechanical – I made use of the 'dictate' and 'read as' functions on my laptop – and deliberative: my choices were quite conscious, though guided by procedure. The process was my old friend, the stochastic. Then I revised the text in an intuitive way, unrecognisable in this latest form. My guide might well have been the proto-surrealist 'formulation' of Lautréamont, in the glorious misquote/typo from a book by Geoffrey Thurley, *The Ironic Harvest* (1974): 'the chance meeting of an umbrella and a sowing-machine on an operating table'!

I did not want to repeat the grim and ghastly scenarios that documentary sources had laid before me; I sought to introduce the main actors into a drama not quite theirs, and not quite mine, either.

I wished to liberate them, albeit imaginatively, from history. I like to think that Keen and Ellis become the positive creative energies to transform this loathsome narrative towards different endings – or none. Those transformations are not just a matter of form, but of a forming of its matters, its matters of fact, and its matters of fiction.

The turn to the 'verse-novel', however ironical, reflects yet another, late, act of transformation, the translation to 'verse', a term I seldom use. These procedures and processes are well described by Derek Attridge in his *The Work of Literature* (2015) when he tells us: 'The coming-into-being of the work of art is ... both an act and an event: it's something the artist does ... and something that happens to the artist.' This work has been hard labour but it has manifested itself before and within me, almost without me.

ACKNOWLEDGEMENTS

The first three chapters were published online in *FreeVoice 37: Surrealist Poetry*, Shuddhashar, Norway, in February 2024.

LAY OUT YOUR UNREST